REPTILES & AMPHIBIANS

CONSTRICTOR SNAKES

Per Christiansen

Gareth Stevens
Publishing

Please visit our web site at **www.garethstevens.com**
For a free color catalog describing Gareth Stevens Publishing's
list of high-quality books, call 1-800-542-2595 (USA)
or 1-800-387-3178 (Canada).
Gareth Stevens Publishing's fax: 1-877-542-2596

Library of Congress Cataloging-in-Publication Data
available upon request from publisher.

ISBN-10: 0-8368-9220-8 (lib. bdg)
ISBN-13: 978-0-8368-9220-8 (lib. bdg.)

This North American edition first published in 2009 by
Gareth Stevens Publishing
A Weekly Reader® Company
1 Reader's Digest Road
Pleasantville, NY 10570-7000 USA

Copyright © 2009 by Amber Books, Ltd.
Produced by Amber Books Ltd., Bradley's Close
74–77 White Lion Street
London N1 9PF, U.K.

Illustrations:
4–13 © Amber Books Ltd.; 14–29 © International Masters
Publishers AB

Project Editor: James Bennett
Design: Tony Cohen

Gareth Stevens Senior Managing Editor: Lisa M. Herrington
Gareth Stevens Editor: Joann Jovinelly
Gareth Stevens Creative Director: Lisa Donovan
Gareth Stevens Designer: Paul Bodley

Printed in the United States of America

2 3 4 5 6 7 8 9 10 09

Contents

Continents of the World

The world is divided into seven continents — North America, South America, Europe, Africa, Asia, Australia, and Antarctica. In this book, the area where each animal lives is shown in red, while all land is shown in green.

Words that appear in the glossary are printed in **boldface** type the first time they occur in the text.

Anaconda

The anaconda is the heaviest snake in the world. Like all **constrictor** snakes, it has a long, powerful body that squeezes its **prey** until they **suffocate**.

The anaconda's skin is a muddy green color with black and brown spots. These colors provide excellent **camouflage** in the warm, wet swamps where it lives. The snake lies underwater and waits for its prey.

Tough scales cover the anaconda's body. The large scales on its underside are used for crawling along the ground.

The anaconda can unhinge its jaws, so the lower jaw separates from the upper jaw. This helps the snake swallow prey that is up to four times its width!

The anaconda is one of the world's largest snakes. Some anacondas grow to a length of 30 feet (9 meters) and can weigh as much as 500 pounds (227 kilograms).

Anacondas are excellent swimmers. They usually live near rivers, lakes, and swamps. The water helps support their heavy bodies. They are extremely strong, but they rarely prey on humans.

1 The anaconda can overpower large prey, such as deer, wild pigs, and even alligators. This anaconda coils around an alligator and slowly suffocates it.

2 The snake unhinges its jaws so its mouth can open extremely wide. Then it swallows the entire alligator! The alligator slowly disappears into the snake's stomach.

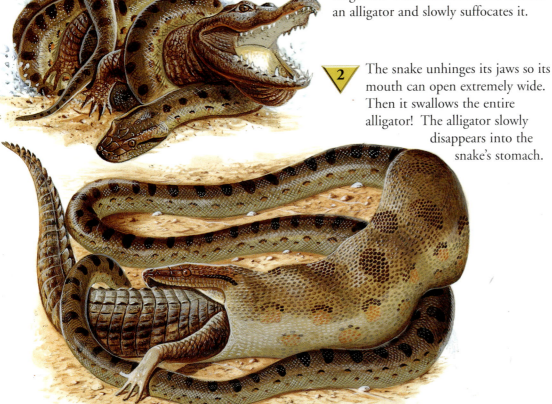

Where in the World

The four **species** of anacondas live in South America. Most are found in the swamps and jungles of the Amazon rain forest.

Boa Constrictor

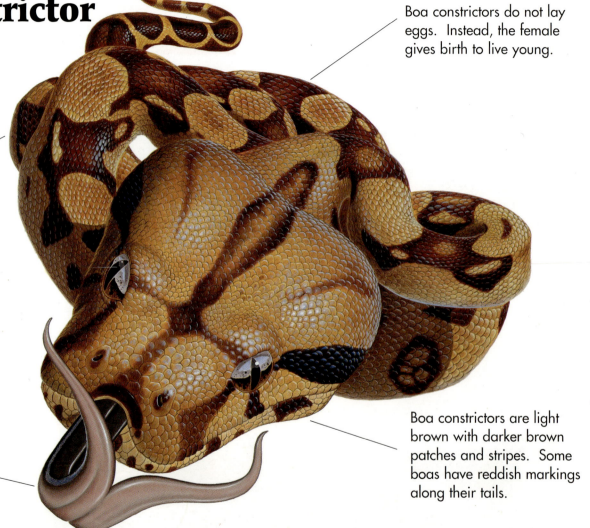

The boa constrictor has a **muscular** body that wraps tightly around its prey. Boa constrictors and pythons are the two main types of constrictor snakes.

Boa constrictors do not lay eggs. Instead, the female gives birth to live young.

Like other snakes, the boa constrictor has a forked tongue. It uses its tongue to pick up scents in the air.

Boa constrictors are light brown with darker brown patches and stripes. Some boas have reddish markings along their tails.

The boa is a medium-sized constrictor snake. Adult boas normally grow to between five feet (1.5 m) and 10 feet (3 m) in length. A 14.5-foot (4.4-m) boa lives at the San Diego Zoo in California.

1 This boa constrictor wraps its coils around a capybara, a large rodent. The boa tightens its grip around the rodent until it suffocates.

2 The boa unhinges its jaws and works them over the rodent's head. Each side of the boa's lower jaw moves forward separately while its teeth grip the prey. Slowly, the boa's skin stretches wider.

3 The boa **contracts** its muscles and expands its ribs. The rodent is pushed into the snake's stomach. The boa will digest its prey in one week.

Where in the World

The boa constrictor lives in Central and South America. It also lives on the Caribbean islands of Trinidad, Tobago, and Dominica.

Indian Python

The Indian python is usually light brown or yellow with dark spots. Some Indian pythons are completely white.

The Indian python has **spurs** near its tail. The python's **ancestor**, which lived millions of years ago, was a lizard with limbs. The spurs are all that is left of what were once the lizard's hind legs.

The Indian python has a large, flat head and big nostrils. It has small eyes and cannot see well.

The scales of a healthy Indian python are smooth and slightly glossy.

Indian pythons are large constrictor snakes. They normally grow no longer than 12 feet (3.7 m), but a 19-foot (5.8-m) python was once found in West Bengal, India! A python that long would weigh 150 pounds (68 kg).

Size

1 The Indian python lives in grasslands, marshes, swamps, and woodlands. Although it moves very slowly, it can catch large prey. It often lies completely still, waiting for prey to come close before it strikes.

2 Indian pythons cannot swallow humans, but these snakes are still dangerous. They have rows of curved, razor-sharp teeth and have been known to bite people.

Did You Know?

All snakes crawl along the ground by contracting their muscles. Anacondas and boa constrictors usually travel in a zigzag pattern. Indian pythons move in a straight line. This way of crawling is slower, but it requires less energy.

Where in the World

Indian pythons live in Southeast Asia. They are found in India, Pakistan, Nepal, Bangladesh, Myanmar (Burma), and parts of China.

9

Reticulated Python

The reticulated python is long and muscular. Unlike other constrictor snakes such as the anaconda, its body is slender.

The snake has bright orange eyes with narrow pupils. It sees well at night.

A "reticulated" pattern looks like a net. This reticulated python gets its name from the net-like pattern on its body. Its color is normally light brown or yellow.

Like other snakes, the reticulated python has a group of sensitive nerve endings inside its mouth. Known together as **Jacobson's organ**, they enable snakes to have a strong sense of smell. The python smells by flicking its forked tongue and then touching its Jacobson's organ to pick up a scent.

Reticulated pythons are huge snakes. They can grow to about 20 feet (6 m). A 32-foot (9.8-m) snake was once caught on the Indonesian island of Sulawesi.

The reticulated python is one of the few constrictor snakes that is dangerous to people. On rare occasions, children and even small adults have been killed and swallowed by giant reticulated pythons!

1 Reticulated pythons that are kept as pets live in **terrariums**, where the temperature and **humidity** can be controlled. They are fed dead chickens or rabbits. This python senses the dead mouse with its forked tongue.

2 The snake keeper dangles the mouse in front of his face. This is a serious mistake! The snake mistakes his face for the dead mouse and strikes!

Where in the World

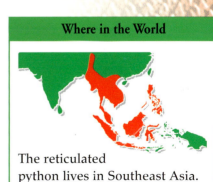

The reticulated python lives in Southeast Asia. It may also be found on many Indonesian islands.

11

Java Wart Snake

The java wart snake's large **windpipe** acts like a second lung. This snake can remain underwater for long periods and can even breathe through its skin!

The java wart snake has loose, baggy skin. This helps it move easily in water but not on land. The java wart snake can breathe through its nostrils while its body is underwater.

Java wart snakes are brown with dark stripes and yellow bellies. Only adult java wart snakes have baggy skin. Young snakes have rigid skin and can travel on land.

The java wart snake's body is covered with small, rough scales. Unlike most adult snakes, the java wart does not have the large scales needed to crawl on land.

Male and female java wart snakes can grow to different lengths. Females are longer than males, reaching about 8 feet (2.4 m). Male snakes rarely grow more than 5 feet (1.5 m).

Size

1 ▶ Java wart snakes live in **brackish** rivers and swamps. They usually live along coasts, but they sometimes swim out to sea.

2 ▶ Java wart snakes feed on fish, but they also eat frogs. They strike with lightning speed. Their sharp teeth hold prey tightly.

3 ▶ The java wart swallows the fish whole. Other snakes have a distinct bulge in their bodies after a large meal, but the java wart shows no such signs.

Where in the World

Java wart snakes live in Southeast Asia. They also live in India and Sri Lanka, as well as on the Indo-Australian islands.

Dumeril's Boa

A long ribcage made up of dozens of ribs forms the body of Dumeril's boa.

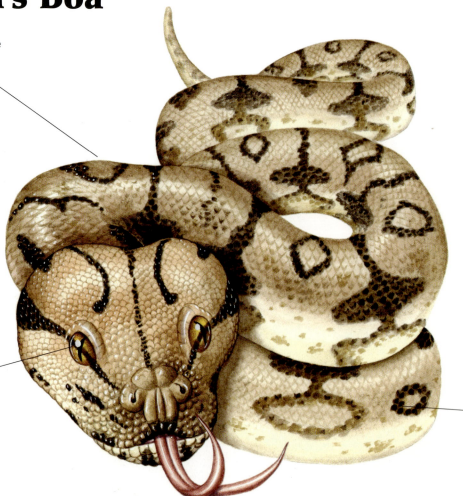

Like many **nocturnal** snakes, Dumeril's boa has vertical, slit-like pupils. It can see well at night.

Dumeril's boa is grayish-brown with dark brown patches. Its colors make great camouflage among the leaves on the forest floor.

Dumeril's boa is a medium constrictor snake. Males can grow to about 5 feet (1.5 m). Females grow longer, reaching between 7 feet (2 m) and 9 feet (2.7m).

Although Dumeril's boa has no **venom**, it can be harmful. It is an aggressive snake, and its mouth is lined with rows of razor-sharp teeth. If Dumeril's boa is bothered, it will give a powerful bite!

1 Dumeril's boa lives on the forest floor, where its color pattern makes it difficult for **predators** to see.

2 During the day, Dumeril's boa lies motionless. At night, it becomes active. The snake preys on small animals, such as mice, rats, birds, lizards, and frogs. It hides so that it can **ambush** its prey.

Where in the World

Dumeril's boa lives in Madagascar, an island off the coast of Africa. Farming destroyed many of the forests where it once lived. Now the snake is found only on the southwestern part of the island.

Calabar Python

The Calabar python's body has a distinctly round shape.

The tail of a Calabar python looks like a head!

The color of the Calabar python can vary. It is usually dark brown or black, with patches of reddish or yellowish-brown scales.

Glossy, smooth scales cover the Calabar python's body. Like many snakes, it has larger, flat scales on its belly. The python uses these larger scales for crawling.

Calabar pythons are among the smallest constrictors. They normally do not grow longer than 3 feet (1 m). Males and females are nearly the same length, though the males are thinner.

Calabar pythons burrow through the soil and dead leaves on the forest floor. They tunnel through the upper layer of soil in search of rodent nests. When they find a nest, they often feed on mice and rats.

1 Like Dumeril's boa, the Calabar python has a color pattern that makes it hard to see among leaves on the forest floor.

2 The Calabar python has an unusual defense against predators. First, it coils its body to protect its head. Next, the python raises its tail and often wiggles it to attract the predator's attention. Finally, the snake strikes.

3 If the predator is not scared off, it will often bite only the python's tail, not its head.

Where in the World

Calabar pythons live in the **tropical** forests of West Africa from Sierra Leone to the Democratic Republic of the Congo.

17

Rubber Boa

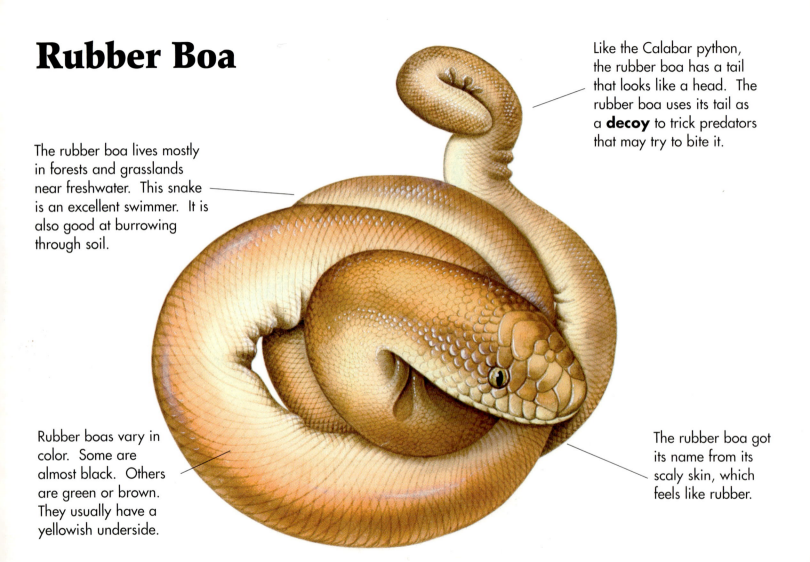

Like the Calabar python, the rubber boa has a tail that looks like a head. The rubber boa uses its tail as a **decoy** to trick predators that may try to bite it.

The rubber boa lives mostly in forests and grasslands near freshwater. This snake is an excellent swimmer. It is also good at burrowing through soil.

Rubber boas vary in color. Some are almost black. Others are green or brown. They usually have a yellowish underside.

The rubber boa got its name from its scaly skin, which feels like rubber.

The rubber boa is a small constrictor snake. It can grow to a length of about 3 feet (1 m). When threatened, the rubber boa protects its head just like the Calabar python does.

Size

Did You Know?

The rubber boa and the rosy boa are the only two types of boa native to the United States. Few people have spotted a rubber boa. The snake is nocturnal and usually stays out of sight.

1 This raccoon has found a rubber boa. The snake will make a tasty meal, but the boa has a plan for survival. First, it curls its body around its head for protection.

2 Then the rubber boa tries to scare the raccoon. The snake lifts its thick tail to attract the raccoon. If the raccoon decides to bite, the snake will not suffer a deadly injury.

Where in the World

Rubber boas live near the U.S. Pacific coast, from California to Oregon. They also live in Idaho, Nevada, Wyoming, and Utah.

Carpet Python

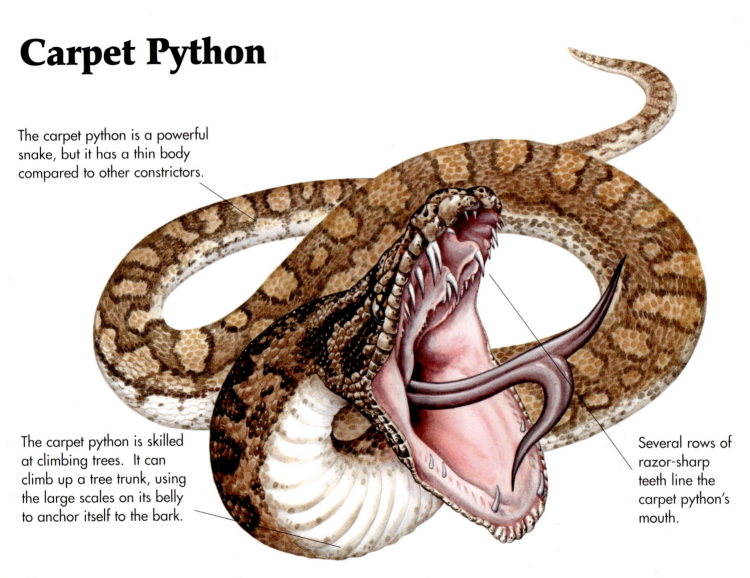

The carpet python is a powerful snake, but it has a thin body compared to other constrictors.

The carpet python is skilled at climbing trees. It can climb up a tree trunk, using the large scales on its belly to anchor itself to the bark.

Several rows of razor-sharp teeth line the carpet python's mouth.

The carpet python is a medium-sized constrictor snake. Males can grow to 6 feet (1.8 m). Females are thicker and longer, often reaching more than 8 feet (2.4 m).

Did You Know?

A female carpet python lays eggs in hidden places, such as hollow logs or holes in trees. The python then coils around the eggs to protect them. The snake even warms the eggs by contracting its large, powerful muscles.

1 Carpet pythons live in many environments, from wooded grasslands to thick jungles. They cannot live in places without trees or bushes.

2 Carpet pythons can be a variety of colors and patterns. They are often beige or brown, with darker patches or stripes. Some are almost pink or yellow. Scientists think these color and pattern varieties are due to **adaptations** that took place over time.

3 The carpet python's colorings provide good camouflage. These snakes often lie for hours, waiting patiently to ambush their prey. They feed on birds and small mammals, especially opossums.

Where in the World

The carpet python lives in much of Australia and New Guinea. There are several closely related types of carpet pythons throughout this region.

21

Black-Headed Python

If black-headed pythons are disturbed in the wild, they will hiss loudly, but they do not normally bite.

The tail of the black-headed python tapers to a thin point.

The black-headed python gets its name from the unusual color of its head. No other species of python looks like this snake!

Black-headed pythons have a tan, light-brown, or yellow color, with rows of darker stripes.

The black-headed python is a medium-sized constrictor. Males are shorter and thinner than females. They can grow to 7 feet (2 m). Females can grow longer than males, often to more than 9 feet (2.7 m).

1 This black-headed female python has laid ten eggs. A group of eggs is called a **clutch**.

2 The python gathers its eggs in a circle and then carefully coils its body around them so they are protected. The python keeps the eggs warm by contracting the muscles in its body. If it left the clutch, the young snakes inside would die.

3 The python stays with its clutch for two to three months, until the tiny young hatch. The young snakes crawl away a few hours after hatching. Then the python can finally eat!

Where in the World

Black-headed pythons live in northern Australia. They are found in forests to grasslands, but they tend to avoid deserts.

Burmese Python

Burmese pythons are yellow or light brown with many dark spots.

Each snake in the giant python group has a distinct design on the top of its head. The Burmese python's head pattern is shaped like a diamond.

Burmese pythons feed on birds, small mammals, and reptiles, but they have the strength to capture larger prey.

The Burmese python is one of the largest snakes in the world. Males can grow to 15 feet (4.6 m), and females may reach 20 feet (6 m).

For many years, giant pythons such as the reticulated python and the Burmese python were killed in huge numbers. People used the pythons' skin to make leather goods. Today these snakes are endangered. It is illegal to kill them or keep them as pets.

1 Burmese pythons are ambush predators. They hide and wait for prey to come close enough to be caught.

2 This Burmese python has waited days for an antelope to come close. The python strikes swiftly, sinking its large, razor-sharp teeth into the antelope's neck. The snake immediately begins coiling its huge, powerful body around the animal. Within minutes, the antelope dies from suffocation.

3 The python will carefully open its mouth until the lower jaw is completely unhinged. Then, it will swallow the antelope whole!

Where in the World

The Burmese python lives in many Asian countries, not just Myanmar (Burma). It also lives in Thailand, Vietnam, China, and Indonesia.

Cuban Wood Snake

Cuban wood snakes are relatives of the boa constrictor. They are sometimes called "dwarf boas."

The scales of most Cuban wood snakes are darkly colored, but some are all one color.

Cuban wood snakes vary in color from gray-brown to yellow with a black-tipped or orange-tipped tail.

The Cuban wood snake is a very small constrictor. Males do not usually grow longer than 2 feet (61 centimeters). Females can grow as long as 3 feet (1 m).

Size

The Cuban wood snake does not lay eggs. Instead, it gives birth to live young. A female usually gives birth to up to ten snakes at once. The young snakes crawl away soon after birth and live on their own.

1 The Cuban wood snake lives on the ground, but it also climbs around in bushes or on rocks. It preys on small lizards and mammals, frogs, and small snakes.

2 The Cuban snake is too small to defend itself by hissing and biting. When threatened by a predator, the snake coils into a tight ball with its head in the center for protection. Then it oozes foul-smelling, sticky **mucus**!

Where in the World

The Cuban wood snake lives on the island of Cuba. It also lives on other Caribbean islands.

Arafura File Snake

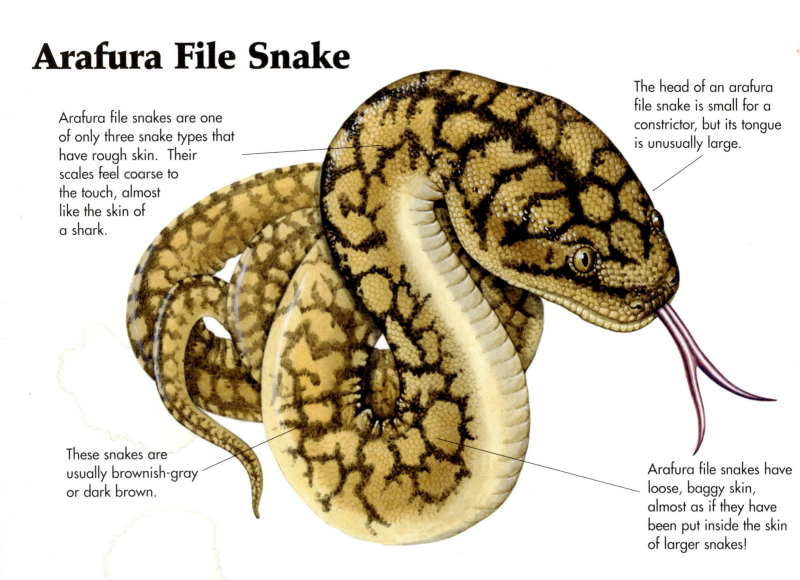

Arafura file snakes are one of only three snake types that have rough skin. Their scales feel coarse to the touch, almost like the skin of a shark.

The head of an arafura file snake is small for a constrictor, but its tongue is unusually large.

These snakes are usually brownish-gray or dark brown.

Arafura file snakes have loose, baggy skin, almost as if they have been put inside the skin of larger snakes!

The arafura file snake is a medium-sized constrictor that lives only in water. Males can reach 6 feet (1.8 m). Females can grow up to 8 feet (2.4 m).

The arafura file snake can stay underwater for long periods. When the snake does come up for air, it can breathe through its skin! The snake's baggy skin provides extra surface area for breathing.

1 Arafura file snakes live in fresh or brackish water in lakes, streams or swamps, and along coastlines. They usually rest on the sandy bottom, often hiding in plant growth while waiting for prey.

2 This snake mostly feeds on fish. It anchors itself to a plant or small rock so it has a stable base from which to strike. The snake attacks with great speed, catching the fish with its sharp teeth. It may even prey on large catfish.

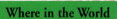

Where in the World

The arafura file snake lives in the wetlands and coastal areas of northern Australia, as well as in New Guinea.

Glossary

adaptations – changes in an animal's body that occurred over time in order to improve its chances of survival

ambush – to make a surprise attack from a hiding place

ancestor – a human or animal that lived in an earlier period of time

brackish – a mix of ocean water and fresh water; salty water

camouflage – colors or patterns on animals that blend in with their surroundings so it is hard to see them

clutch – a group of animal eggs

constrictor – a snake that kills its prey by coiling around it squeezing it until it suffocates

contracts — tightens or draws together

decoy – something used as a lure

endangered — at risk of dying out

humidity – the amount of water in the air

Jacobson's organ – an organ in a snake's mouth that it uses to pick up a scent

Latin – the language of the ancient Romans, which scientists use to name plants and animals

mucus – a thick, jellylike liquid made by an animal to protect its body

muscular — having a lot of muscle, the material that gives a body strength

nocturnal – being active during the night instead of during the day

predators – animals that hunt and kill other animals for food

prey – animals that predators hunt and eat

species – a group of living things of the same type

spurs – stiff, sharp spines that project from the body of an animal

suffocate – die from not being able to breathe

terrariums – places for keeping snakes and other land animals

tropical – referring to the hottest regions of the world, with lush plant life and a lot of rain

venom – a poison that a snake puts into its prey when it bites

windpipe – the tube in a body through which air travels from the throat to the lungs

For More Information

Books

Anacondas. Snakes (series). Linda George.
(Edge Books, 2001)

The Best Book of Snakes. The Best Book of (series).
Christiane Gunzi (Kingfisher, 2006)

Boa Constrictors. World's Largest Snakes (series).
Valerie J. Weber (Gareth Stevens, 2002)

Deadly Snakes. Wild Predators (series). Andrew Solway
(Heinemann Library, 2004)

Red-tailed Boas and Relatives. Reptile Keeper's Guides
(series). R. D. Bartlett and Patricia Bartlett (Barron's
Educational Series, 2003)

The Snake Book. Chris Mattison (DK, 2006)

Web Sites

Anaconda – Kids Encyclopedia
www.4to40.com/encyclopedia/index.asp?id=576

Boa Constrictor Fact Sheet – Smithsonian National Zoo
*nationalzoo.si.edu/Animals/ReptilesAmphibians/Facts/Fact
Sheets/Boaconstrictor.cfm*

Boa – Kids Encyclopedia
www.4to40.com/encyclopedia/index.asp?id=578

Burmese Profile – National Geographic
*science.nationalgeographic.com/animals/reptiles/burmese-
python.html*

Constrictors Unlimited
www.constrictors.com

The UnMuseum – Big Snakes
unmuseum.mus.pa.us/bigsnake.htm

Index